Also by David McKee

Elmer
Elmer and Rose
Elmer and the Rainbow
Elmer's Christmas
Elmer's Special Day

American edition published in 2010 by Andersen Press USA, an imprint of Andersen Press Ltd.
www.andersenpressusa.com

First published in Great Britain in 2003 by Andersen Press Ltd., 20 Vauxhall Bridge Road,
London SW1V 2SA. Published in Australia by Random House Australia Pty.,
20 Alfred Street, Milsons Point, Sydney, NSW 2061.

Distributed in the United States and Canada by
Lerner Publishing Group, Inc.
241 First Avenue North
Minneapolis, MN 55401 U.S.A.
www.lernerbooks.com

Library of Congress Cataloging-in-Publication Data Available.

ISBN: 978-0-7613-6442-9

Color separated in Switzerland by Photolitho AG, Zürich.
Printed and bound by TWP, Singapore.
This book has been printed on acid-free paper.
2 – TWP – 2/11/11

ELMER
and the HIPPOS

David McKee

Andersen Press USA

Elmer, the patchwork elephant, was having a friendly chat with Lion and Tiger when three angry elephants came by.

"Elmer," said one, "the hippos have come to live here."

"Tell them to to go, Elmer," said the second. "There isn't room for them and us."

"What if they don't want to go?" asked Elmer.

"Tell them we'll make them," said the third elephant.

"Hmmm," said Elmer. "Let me talk to them."

"Hello, Hippos," said Elmer.
"Hello, Elmer," said the hippos.
"Elmer," said one, "we know we're not wanted here,
but our river has dried up and we have to have a river."
"Make yourself at home," said Elmer. "I'll speak to
the elephants."

Elmer told the elephants about the hippos'
problem. "Imagine if our river dried up," he said.
The elephants agreed to let the hippos stay but
grumbled because the river would be crowded.
"I'll take a look at their river," said Elmer.

The hippos' river was completely dry.
"Strange," thought Elmer. "I wonder what happened?"
He set off along the dry riverbed.

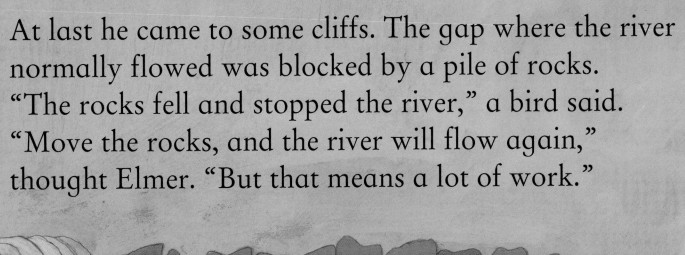

At last he came to some cliffs. The gap where the river normally flowed was blocked by a pile of rocks. "The rocks fell and stopped the river," a bird said. "Move the rocks, and the river will flow again," thought Elmer. "But that means a lot of work."

On his way home, Elmer visited his cousin, Wilbur.
"Come on, Wilbur," he said. "I need your help."

"Good," said the elephants when they heard the news. "The hippos can move the rocks, get their river back, and go home."

"It will take them ages," said Wilbur. "They don't have trunks. Still, they can stay here and use our river. . . ."

An elephant said, "If we help, it will soon be done."

"Right," said Elmer. "Get a good night's sleep. We'll start early in the morning."

The next morning, Elmer called the hippos.
"Come on, we're going to get your river back. Are you feeling strong?"

The elephants and hippos were soon bragging about how strong they were as they marched along.

When they saw the rocks, the bragging stopped and they set to work, pushing and pulling the rocks from the gap.

As the pile became smaller, the elephants and the hippos all became dustier.

"I'd love a nice dip in the river now," said an elephant.

"Keep working, and you'll soon be able to," laughed Elmer.

Some time later, a hippo shouted,
"Water!" as the first trickle came
through the rocks.
"Careful," said Wilbur. "It will come
with a rush."

It did.
The water suddenly poured through, pushing the last of the
rocks out of the way.

Cheering and laughing, they all plunged into the river and forgot their tiredness as they washed off the dust and played in the water.

When they finally parted, the hippos thanked the elephants
and said, "Come and visit us anytime."
"You too," said the elephants. "Anytime!"

Later, Elmer said, "You were all pretty friendly with the hippos in the end."
"Of course," said an elephant. "Besides, imagine if our river dried up?"